MISSIONS

What a fascinating conversation
with a lovely stranger!
I hope you enjoy!

Mark Needham

MISSIONS

War and Windmills
Second Edition

MARK NEEDHAM

TATE PUBLISHING
AND ENTERPRISES, LLC

Missions

Published by Tate Publishing & Enterprises, LLC
127 E. Trade Center Terrace | Mustang, Oklahoma 73064 USA
1.888.361.9473 | www.tatepublishing.com

Tate Publishing is committed to excellence in the publishing industry. The company reflects the philosophy established by the founders, based on Psalm 68:11,
"The Lord gave the word and great was the company of those who published it."

Cover design by Jennifer Schrider and Mark Needham
Interior design by Mary Jean Archival

Published in the United States of America

ISBN: 978-1-62563-324-8
1. Fiction / Action & Adventure
2. Fiction / Visionary & Metaphysical
13.05.21

This book is dedicated to my little brother,

Tyler

CONTENTS

Introduction

I had a dream. It was unlike any dream I have ever had before. I was sitting by a lake wondering how I had got there. My awareness of my circumstances would have faded except, there was something strange about the whole thing. The world was different. The colors were brighter, the textures were sharper. There was something about it that gave me a sustained euphoric feeling. I realized it was a dream at this point; though I realized something else that confounded me. I came to the realization that this place was *more real* than the waking hours I had endured for so many years. It was not static. It was not mundane. It was influential and fluid. And you were there, and we were best friends. I had such a profound love for you, even though this was the first time I thought I had met you. We began to realize we had gone through so much together somewhere long ago. We had done so many things to each other and ourselves, terrible things. Though it didn't matter because those days were gone and we understood much more than we did then. Oddly enough, we were ecstatic that we had done these terrible things. Because it made us strong, it made us wise. If the dream were to continue, we would build worlds together. We'd make new rules. We'd watch things grow, fight and love. And we would continue doing this for eternity or until we discovered a deeper truth. Until we began to see an even stranger horizon. A terrifying and exciting one. And we would be brave. We would immerse ourselves in the waters of uncertainty. And it would be perfect, forever.

When I awoke, I had the funny feeling that I figured it all out. Everything. Why we are here, how we got to Earth, everything. I rested with this notion for a time. After this time spent, I knew exactly what I had to do.

— L.

MISSIONS

MISSION 1

ALPHA: COL. JACOB RIVERS REPORTING...

"There's a storm coming." I spoke the obvious. "I know," my brother said. I laugh a little inside. He always knew. He knew of every storm, every skirmish, and every enemy. He knew the answer to every problem of every homework assignment. Every night I missed my mother and my sister, he knew what to say, what to do. He is my father, my uncle and my best friend. Most of all, he is my big brother. He is the reason I am still alive amidst this chaos. He has saved my life countless times and taken countless lives to do so. I hope that one day, I can return the favor.

I am Colonel Jacob Rivers, son of Mark the unknown warrior, the deadbeat father. I am an eighteen year old colonel, who, like my father and brother, kill men for a living. I like video games, vacations at the beach and the sound of gunfire. I killed a man when I was fifteen. I didn't feel a morsel of remorse or sadness. I just remember how much I liked the power. How much better it was than a video game. This kill promoted me to the rank I am today. I am a well decorated soldier in the Anti-Federalist National militia lead by the great Saul Rivers. Saul, my brother, is the general of our militia. He too shares the Y in his chromosome with the unknown warrior. He too likes the sound of gunfire, though he does not so much enjoy killing. Honestly, he hates it. He has a pride though, and he was proud of every being he murdered because that death stemmed from something righteous for him. My brother says: "You must never have a mind for war, only a mind for survival. Though if war comes as a result of your pursuit for survival, so be it. That is something worth fighting for." He believes this is how we remain true humans sustained in our virtue. These words he spoke have always stuck in my head. These words represent the place where me and my brother coexist and have something in common. And that is where it ends. He is much more like the Samurai of Japan, the Monks of Tibet maybe. I am an American Warrior. I am ruthless, rash and unforgiving. When life allows, my brother is kind, thoughtful, and soft in his demeanor. Though when he is threatened, when he is opposed, he is diabolical, treacherous and so he is surprising and unpredictable. He is my hero and my antagonist. He is the latter because he is not like me. He has a heart even after all of this. Though, in my defense it makes sense to a degree. He had time to conserve his heart. He was a grown man when the war started, while I was still so young. I couldn't even drive a car yet and my brother was trying to show me how to load and cock a shotgun. "The shotgun is a perfect all-purpose weapon, incredible accuracy, heavy round, deadly close quarter killing capacity." Saul always spoke like a true soldier even before he became one. He had me in the same boots, walking the same way, the Hoorah, the trumpets and bagpipes. So I think about it, after all this, how does it make me feel?

Well I got it in me. To fight, to kill, to pillage and burn… Fortunately for us all, he doesn't. It just sits with him for a time, and when it lacks necessity, it will leave him just like that. My brother is a true leader and a man of peace, so as far as we are all concerned, a stranger in a strange land. 'Moses of America'. Regardless of that, we remain at the top of the food chain. No one messes with us. Our mentality and our motto is, if a man steps to us, he can get it, and die by our hands. As they do, every time.

MISSION 1

BRAVO: GENERAL SAUL RIVERS REPORTING...

"There's a storm coming" my brother says nervously... I know why he says it. He says it because there is nothing else to say. He says it because on the other side of that mountain is a very terrifying enemy. Something I'm not afraid to say I'm afraid of. I say in a calming tone, "I know." He smiles. I know him knowing I have control over the situation makes him feel safe and at home. Like Sunday dinners at moms. Even when it is just a matter of meteorology, it matters. Every bit of information I am aware of and every bit concealed for which I don't, adds to the illusion that I am in complete control, all-knowing of the purpose at hand. Though he is not naïve by any means, he makes an effort to be ignorant for the sake of his own sanity. He is a wise young man and a decent soldier at only eighteen, though he might as well be my age. For what he has seen, is a lifetime's worth of sights. These things that have arrived to him visually, physically, make him quick on his feet and with his head. He is full of pride, bravery and arrogance. The perfect disposition of a great warrior destined for a legend of audacity for his foes, ink in history, and a young death. For his sake, I love him to death and I would make death so that he could live. I protect him, and so justify everything that he is.

We sit prone in some tall grass. It's foggy, a light fog so subtle it almost isn't there, meandering beautifully with a light rain. Despite the fog you can still see the green all around. We rest on the shortest of three hills which could almost make for mountains. The other two are parallel to one in which we reside on. I just stare out a bit and look at the green of the trees. As the wind passes through this small ravine, you see the invisible giant. It touches the foliage, changing the shades of green. First a light pale green as the winds cuts across and lifts up the leaves a bit, exposing the underside of them, then I see the wonderful shade of emerald I am so accustomed to as it whips down the hill forcing the leaves downward, putting strain on the stems and branches. Up and down the wind passes, dancing through the trees. This is so lovely to me. I am sentimental. Upstate New York is my home. A wonderful place to rest your head, and so a terrible place to wage war.

"Old soul and young blood
Mortar shells and evergreens
Stir in my spirit"

From our Current position, I can see the two windmill projects in the area that are southwest of Utica. That puts us in the general vicinity of Oriskany Falls and Madison.

Thirty minutes and three years from where and when I lived a normal, and in its own respect, exciting life. Not as exciting as the three years that followed though... Ask me if I would trade it in. The blood and tears, the relatives and loves lost to savage acts of friend and foe. In the midst of this, a living legend I had become. And for what? I Question my desire in all of this, what is it worth to me? Why I never ran or hid. How I came to lead an entire army. God we've come so far from the Community. So many strange things have happen to us. Things I wouldn't even believe in had they not happened. Just looking back blows my mind—the stars could not predict this. What a story I have to tell. It was supposed to be about peace and the virtues of man. Ended up being about war and vices...It will all start to make more sense soon I promise. I won't be able to keep you in the dark, though I doubt in the eve of realization you will see any light.

We're taking a break from it all for a few hours. Thankfully we are able to find refuge in what all battling parties agree is a neutral zone. The Crimson and we like to call it 'The Holy Land'. We decided that something should be sacred. That when this was all over the victor would need somewhere to call home. Ironically, this little patch of land with modest boundaries is in the most highly disputed ground in America, besides the eastern bay itself. This area, which is located in approximately in the middle of New York, is part of what we all like to call the "choke hold" district. Strategically, if you control the choke hold, you control the eastern bay, which is the only place our allies will drop anchor to resupply us. If you have the choke hold your ally is shipping. You lose the choke, you lose resupply and your opponent gets the drops. Now what is left of the American government and its military has all of its resources from before the war and has no allies to speak of. But the Union isn't the only tribe throwing spears. The Crimson Army has its roots in this war as well. The Crimson is what lies on the other side of those hills. They're exhausting, and I don't want to talk about them right now.

The windmills are so amazing to me. They're like peaceful alien robots with incredible strength. With the majesty to only use it for good. There is such a strange and breathtaking feeling I get when I get close to them. It's hard to look at them as the spin with the wind. Their existence seems impossible yet, there they are. I wonder about their mystic nature. Is it because they are so foreign to my everyday life that they move me so? Or is there something truly enigmatic emanating from the source of these inanimate beings? I would love to be able to answer these questions. At this point, I would love if these were all the thoughts of my mind in a day. I could spend every day for God knows how long just taking this place in. Maybe I could answer that question, what is grass? I would do it for Walt Whitman. I might write a book about it. Call it *Windmills and Waterfalls, Life before Death.* Though for now, I am indefinitely destined to follow my heart through this insane conquest, like Don Quixote himself. Me and you Don, why do we do this to ourselves? And what do we see in these windmills that no one else does? Everything around me is responsible for a story, for a stirring in someone's heart who thought kindly and bravely enough to write about it. Walt is in the grass, Miguel de Cervantes Saavedra in the windmills. Who is in the sky though? Who completes this thought? Albert is there, wondering about everything else in the universe, knowing why the sky is blue, and not green.

If my story were written, the bloodshed, the war and tears, what would it really mean? Just as it appears to be? A savage story of men with no conscience. *Or would the author know to tell my story for what it truly is?* I think the author would make it clear to his reader, that there is so much to my story that will not present itself so instantaneously. If you want instant gratification or revelation, read a romance novel, my story would not be for you. However, if you search for something enlightening, something that will fill your soul over time, I believe I would be capable of that… We'll if I we're a character in a story I could. I think there is still hope for me, and a lovely story to tell. So don't be afraid or lose your appetite when the guns come out, because violence never ends, not in this life unfortunately. And unfortunately, I feel the violence upon me. It will be here soon, and will not stop. In the end though, it will all mean something more important than the primer igniting the gunpowder, hurling hot lead at unfortunate flesh. It will be about something, *something worth fighting for*. It will be a story of what human beings are capable of, good and bad, and how both matter. How both are beautiful elements of our condition as cognitive, rational, and sometimes irrational beings trying to escape both being animal, and something more. Lost between two pivot points like black holes, afraid to fall into either; wondering which one is the better choice, the better life.

"Are we animals—Or Gods?"—"POP!"

"Whoa!" I yell in automatic response.

"What?" My brother asks nervously.

"Get down!" I scream at him.

That loud pop tells me I am foolish for wandering in my head. That I am foolish for thinking somebody wouldn't take back their promise. And most importantly, it tells me my wandering head almost exploded from a 50 caliber bullet. It's gotta be a Barrett. It came from the across the valley. My intuition, guided by logic tells me the shot came from the left side of the hill.

"Have you no honor in your heart!? Everybody get down!" I roar like a lion. "Load the mortars, fire when I give the ready!" My voice carries all the way down the mountainside. As it does everyone hits the dirt like a wave as they hear the sound of my voice, like a human sound wave flowing down the mountain.

"The Crimson wouldn't snipe." my brother states curiously. He's right. The Crimson wouldn't watch me die from a distance. They love to be close.

"Yea, I know, but what would the Union be doing here?! Doesn't make any sense! What do you think?!

"It's got to be them; they would be the only ones using Barrett M82s' besides us!"

It's Union then, hopefully… The important difference it would make if it was Crimson, is a completely different strategy in how were about to kill everything on that mountainside.

So if my brother and I are right, today is a good day to spill some shanty soldier blood. That sniper is probably kicking himself for that half inch. I hope he's terrified because he realizes who he just missed. You almost ended the war buddy, but you also broke one of my rules. You are a coward who shoots from *Deep Cover*. So I will find you, un*cover* you and bury my knife *deep* inside your heart. For any man who uses his bow and arrow better damn well hit his target so that there is no story to tell of his cowardice.

They're loading the mortars behind me, waiting for me to give the orders. I can't think of a better moment than now. You see you came in at a interesting time. We have been fighting this war for years now and we have begun to see the trap we have placed ourselves in. We take this bunker today, they take it tomorrow. We find weapons here, they find weapons there. It will go on forever playing by the orthodox rules of war. So I have devised a plan, I have decided to break the rules.

"Okay! Listen up!" I turn my back to the ground still lying prone as I prepare to give the most important speech of this campaign in the most unfavorable of bodily positions. God must be proud of my faith… Or ashamed of my arrogance.

"Pass this through the valley to all the soldiers so I can be heard crisply by each and every one of you! This is Mission One. Everything we have done so far is not in vain; it was simply the vehicle that has delivered us to the final stretch of this war! And so nothing—nothing amounts to Mission One! Because Mission One puts us in position for Mission Two, which will lead us closer and closer to the end! The result will be the ratification of the vile plague that is our enemy; and our boots resting at the foot of the capital raising our flag, celebrating the conquering of the United States of America!—Now fire those mortars!"

I smile at my soldiers, as they smile back with a look of fire in the openness of their grins. The glaze in their eyes scream to me a feeling of belief. They have waited for this speech for a very long time. They have heard the whispers of a special operation being forged away in my mind and in my heart. They have been patient and now they know. It is time to finish this. I feel their hearts, as my heart feels like it's about to explode out of my chest into a million pieces of fleshy confetti in anticipation for the end, and anxiety to live up to the connotation of what a Mission truly means now.

"What do the mortars do men?!" I ask with a sarcastic, smug smile.

"Smoke out the enemy, Drive out the archers!" They speak in crisp, coherent unity.

You see when those hollow tip frag shells start hitting the ground on their hillside, the snipers must run, they are a precious commodity. I assume whoever shot at me was very special, or he wouldn't have been shooting at me. Now they have lost their advantage on my hillside. And as we make our next succession of moves upon them, starting with grenade cans and following with heavy round gunfire, their position on us radically dissipates, so quickly that they are consumed before they realize they are being eaten. I would call for my snipers, but all my men are snipers, as all my men make up three person mortar teams, tank operators, heavy gunners, assassins, we are all specialized specialists four thousand strong.

My brother brings me my rifle, with four men and himself all with their binoculars out.

"Find that sniper!" My brother barks as if they had done something wrong by not finding him already. As I stare at him with his arm outstretched pointing one finger to the hillside across, I see the many mortars being shot off behind him; his voice gets tuned out until his mouth makes inaudible movements. Must be close to fifty teams, loading, plugging their ears, puff of smoke, "phloomp phloomp phloomp!" That's all I can hear and the sight and sound create a feeling in me that makes me feel like some kind of ferocious beast. Yet I also feel like a man. A man leading the most elite and virtuous men of life and war as he prepares to take the high ground of an uncertain enemy. Their advantages of cover and height begin to ring of redundancy in my head as I go over it with an unnecessary caution.—"Saul!" My brother breaks my daze "Yea, what's up?" I say in an unfitting tone. My brother looks at me as if I lost my mind for a moment and says: "We found him, you ready?"

I pull my gun up and look down the scope. My brother immediately adjusts the scope and the gun for me as he says, "You see him, there under those pines with the broken down tree?" "I see him." I reply after a little looking. I see him and his spotter, close together crouched behind the log, motionless, probably praying the mortars don't claim their vital organs. I wonder if they're praying to God. I pull the trigger on the spotter right through both sides of his chest. If he's lucky, I tagged his heart, but I don't think he is. "OOOOOOOOOH!" All five of my men groan in a sick, satisfied sort of way like watching a surfer wipe out on a wave. I quickly release air out of my lungs, which signifies, unlike my victim, mine still work. "Confirm kill." I order. "He ain't dead yet, but he will be." Captain Travino says: "Poor bastard should have never laid his eyes on me" I say in a lamenting tone. Still looking through my scope, I see the sniper making a run for it. My bullet, his knee cap and he's down. I give the other knee cap equal treatment. That's how I'll have him, little wounded fodder. I check for my knife and called my brother. "Yes sir!" He responds as if he needed to behave like a subordinate. A trait that always comes with any skirmish, a trait I admire in him.I would like to say something more on Captain Zachary Travino. He has a kind, timid soul, so, in this life, he has a restless one. Though braver then any man I have ever met when it meant a person dear was in danger. He is something of a man that is ideal, a model for any soldier. When I met him, he was a lost young man not unlike me. Together we have grown like vines wrapped around this life like a stone, as we bear fruit to a dead world. I have grown very fond of him. He reminds me so much of myself. I love my brother, and he comes first, but my brother will forsake me, has forsaken me. Zachary will not. It is not within him to do so. God must have fashioned him an angel and let him loose to wreak havoc upon troubled insecure souls with his inherent goodness. The first thing I ever closely examined was his eyes as they looked upon one of these troubled souls pointing a gun at him. His eyes showed me something special. He had no fear. He was simply hurt that someone would think to pull a gun on him on such an occasion. I was afraid when he looked at me. I'm sure he saw that fear, and so he must have known that man would have killed him; for I knew this to be true. It showed in my eyes like something was pouring out of them I'm sure.

"Were taking the valley in two minutes, "Throw a decoy" I say.

"There's another sniper?"

"Maybe, probably not, better safe than sorry."

He puts up a painted mannequin head with a helmet just slightly in view for the other hillside to see.

Standard Operating Procedure: Dummy Head

In times of uncertainty for your enemy, a Dummy Head is used to extract lethal fire from your assailant. Two minutes on the clock after last shot fired or initial placement. If no shots are fired as of two minutes of initial placement, the all clear is given and the soldiers involved can proceed as per protocol.*

**Aggressive cover fire is mandatory for a Dummy Head procedure.*

He places a mortar cannon in sight with the mannequin. If any sharpshooters see it they will fire upon it. He fires the round and I set my watch. Two minutes—two long minutes.

MISSION 1

CHARLIE: COL. JACOB RIVERS REPORTING...

It's intense; it's always so intense for me, no matter how many times we do it. My blood is hot in my veins. I load another mortar and fire. The sound gives me chills all over my body. You know that feeling you get when you're cold and you get in a warm bath? Like that, but with a taste of fear and courage wrapped in the whole mess. I'm not completely content though, because we should have used the incendiary rounds. My brother knows this, but he won't allow the forest to burn. That's another difference between me and him. You see the trees will grow again, men will not. The fire created will provide us with maximum coverage on the dangerous ascent uphill, which saves lives.

Even though I am colonel of this regiment, he is still the general, so basically he is always right. And even though I don't agree with him much, I wait for the result. I don't have the foresight he has; so many times he satisfies me in the end. Sometimes I'm amazed.

Anyway, the round we're using instead is incredible, it's like a giant hollow tip bullet filled with tiny iron ball bearings. It is death, wrapped in death. My brother came up with the design and his "friend" manufactured and shipped. His friend is one of the fundamental reasons we are so well supplied.

I fire another round. One minute-forty-five seconds, no shots fired. I start checking my M4A1 and turn to see my brother taking the safety off of his M16. It is an unspoken agreement that me and my brother's tools accent each other, making a two man army. *Two Minutes*. They accent each other because although all the soldiers fight as a unit, there is another unit, a more important one: Me and my big brother. Regardless of what happens to anyone else in the world, regardless of how deeply I feel for my people, my brother and I must remain in the end, foremost. The M4A1 Carbine: small round, rapid fire, automatic wounding weapon with short range shotgun attachment. Two Beretta 9MM pistols with a distance upgrade for increased accuracy and range. M16 762mm rifle for him: Long range, heavy round, burst fire killing weapon with frag attachment; medium range explosive device. His secondary Weapon: Barrett M82 sniper rifle. This gun is like a beautiful sports car, and my brother is a professional driver. We get off the mound and call to our captains: "Ready all troops for a full wave!" we both say in a staggered manner. A full wave is an up and down, or down and up through a valley. We dealt with valleys a lot, we needed a name. I look at my brother and he looks at me. "I'm A with you" I say, as I always say. He looks down at his gun and pulls the pin. "Forever?" he says: "For the rest of our time?" he adds. I smile and mimic him, pulling my pin. "Until we're really hurt and they put us in the dirt!" I say and we hurdle the mound and make our descent! Our camp follows with a cry of war that shakes the mountainside! They hear us roar, we cry for their blood.

MISSION 1

DELTA: GEN. SAUL RIVERS REPORTING...

He wants to burn that whole mountainside. In matters that concern death, he is correct in his desire. Unfortunately for him, my desire is to not desecrate the home I plan to make for us after the war. The home that once sustain many of our families. We owe it to the land and more importantly we owe it to God. I'm also thinking ahead now because a speedy date has been put on this war...

What this war has done to this country is not something any man can measure. Hundreds of millions of people have died, mostly civilians looking for something to believe in, partially a people who never saw it coming, who in its wake were just trying to survive. That didn't matter to the war, to our government, to the Crimson. It only seemed to matter to us. That's what always made it so hard. Heartlessness was never our strong suit.

Something else that the war didn't seem to care about was the rest of the world. The war touched everything. It brought down entire empires without pointing a single weapon in their direction. China no longer exists as its own country. It would seem that even though they appeared to have us by the necks and pocketbooks, *the consumer does have all the power.*

When the war started, America went in to complete lock down, total isolationism. China's economy imploded so fiercely that it became in debt itself, and was rationed off to several countries, mainly Great Britain and Russia. America fell deeper still. All her allies severed their ties, washed their hands of the mother who saved them countless times. We were left to eat each other or die. Until The Eurasian United, the new super alliance, made up of everything from Ireland to Japan above the equator, Governed by Russia and the Brits, spoke up. In a statement made available to the international public, they said: "Any nation to seek gain on American soil would be at war with The Eurasian United."

I got a smoke signal a week later. I'm sure the Union and the Crimson received similar calls. It was a deal, and the deal was that America would be protected for two years. In those two years the war had to end, and government had to be reestablished. I'm sure there would be *a catch in the end.* A deal so fair had to stink. But I didn't smell it yet, and I had been limping in on every battle since the beginning, dragging my morals with me. This gave me a reason, maybe even a justification to kill and destroy what I had avoided killing and destroying before. Death it would seem comes to be the only option left available in my arsenal. An arsenal I always prided on being vast enough to overshadow the easily executed form of war known as murder. Sadly, these are much different times. This is 2017 for God's sake, what are we doing still using words! We should be behaving like animals!

I will become the snake. I will creep and find my prey deep in their holes of ignorance and pride. I will eat them all—Mass euthanasia.

The
Devil
Crept to
Man and
Said, "You're
Inherent with sin,
Your blood runs red"
He tears at their skin
And shows this truth,
"You think your angels,
far and few" Man says
"You're just a speaking
Snake; I'd take your
life with fists I make"
The snake replies
"I have no form,
I take this shape,
This makes me perfect
Makes me great,
I have No equal,
God is blind"
With that,
World
with

Devil,
us
m
e
n
r
e
s
i
d
e

"I'm with you" my brother says. I'm taken back, reminds me of a song. "Forever? For the rest of time?" I say with sincere jest. He smiles and says: "Until we get real hurt and they put us in the dirt!" With those words we are almost instantly running down the mountain, screaming at the top of our lungs. I want to scream louder. I'm so overwhelmed with emotion I have to gasp for air. Everyone behind me is loud enough to drown me out so that I can't hear my own words as they come wailing out of my mouth three inches from my ears. It's me and my brother up front with a heavy arms squad twenty feet behind. Rapid fire heavy machine guns are in constant fire over my head. I look to the other side on the enemies hill. I see everything get ripped apart and fall to pieces. Time goes slow now... as it often does when we go hot. I take a deep breath and look around a bit. I focus in on a maple tree that is still untouched by bullets. I look at one of its branches as two bullets pass through one of the trees leaves, leaving two holes with stress fractures from the impact down to the tip of the leaf. After the bullets pass through the large maple leaf, they hit the trunk of the tree and bark comes hurling past the leaf in my direction. This vision broadens to much of the landscape. Bark in pounds of tiny splinters like sawdust rain over the valley like a downpour without a cloud to claim it. Still so slow... I can see small splinters of bark somersaulting through the air. Small trees fall on the bodies of lifeless soldiers rolling down the hill. A faint boom, that is accented by a pink mist and screams awakens me from my trance. I look behind me to see my frag men firing right on cue, uninterrupted by enemy fire. I see them all angle their guns toward the hill moving in a slow jog behind the heavy gunners who are throwing their guns over their backs and reaching for sub machine guns and assault rifles. Captain Travino yells "One, two, three, four!" The way a drummer would announce a song, and there they go. All the canisters, all at once. A hundred little puffs of smoke leave the guns and fill out the air as my men passed through the smoke from their guns that behaves like a thick fog, wrapping around their bodies as they passed through it swirling and dancing about their bodies. I follow the canisters as they arc overhead; leaving light trails like gray snakes in the sky… so beautifully…Everything speeds back up and the canisters hit the mountainside, with vicious intent. I can see the death before I hear the boom. My senses confuse me. I know it can be explained scientifically, but it doesn't feel right, dying without a sound. Nevertheless it makes me feel safe.

Thought it also makes me feel sadness. Thank God it still makes me sad.

How could I be sad and content about something simultaneously? About death of all things? I've come so far since *The Community*. The things I'll do for a better life for me and my brother. Violence for peace.

We run faster and hit the bottom hard. My brother and I take the lead again as some of our men switch to shotguns and unsheathe their scythes; which are modified for climbing. "Shing, shing, shing!" I can hear them unsheathing for a minute as I make my way up the mountainside. R.P.D.'s stop firing. The soldiers with shotguns come up in front of us and begin firing through the dense brush. Soldiers with assault rifles come out from behind the shotgun squad and begin aggressively hiking the valley shooting as they go. "Boom! Boom!" The shotguns pound like a heavy drum, the assault rifles pop like cymbals and snares. I think back to Travino yelling "One, two, three, and four!" All the drums playing, my men's voices scream-ing like violins, guitars and bass. The whole thing is like a musical…

It's funny. It's like a strange metaphor. The audience buys their tickets, thinking it's a show worth watching, a show they will survive. Although they never leave the theater on any occasion. Yet, a new audiences comes every week in hordes, thinking they can prevent the climax. Throw your tomatoes hecklers, we've toured the country and never had to cancel a show!

We slow our ascent to a crawl. I look for my assailant. Breaking from the group, I look back and see my brother on my six. "Take out your Spartan shield," I say: "We're going reckless!"

S.O.P.: Going Reckless

In times of complete insanity in a soldier's mind in the form of several excuses including but not excluded to; "Finishing the fight," "Taking away shame," "Settling a debt," "I have a better idea," or any others, a soldier must be considered 'Going Reckless'." These common phrases are a sure sign a soldier has lost his mind and therefore is wrongfully breaking from a formation. In this situation it is better to embrace the insanity with special precaution instead of attempting to thwart the insane soldier's plans. Mandatory precautions are as follows: Always accent the insane soldier's compromised mentality with a sane one. Do not engage in their plan; instead engage in your own plan of protecting him and yourself. And most importantly, SPARTAN SHIELD UP AT ALL TIMES DURING THE CORRUPTED SOLDIER'S EPIC OF INSANITY!

Going Reckless was straying from the plan. You only strayed from the plan when a man had made an attempt at your life and failed miserably. Because you are still alive, you are aware of the shame he tried to bring upon you, and that he is now full of shame himself. This is a heavy weight to carry, so as always, you must kill this man and relieve...his... burden...

I don't look back at my brother; it would be too dangerous to lose sight of what's in front of me. "Is your shield up?" I yell. "I'm fine." he says with what he thinks is the confidence of a decorated military man, but it is really the arrogance of a young buck. "Put it up now, that's an order!" I scream, mostly from how excited I am in my situation, less because I am actually angry. God, when I get like this, when I feel crazy, you must be sane brother. I must do this, so you need to anchor me, at least with sound judgment for yourself. This is all Luther's fault you know, him and his stupid 'Magical' blade! It makes me sick thinking about it. One day it will drive him insane, right before it kills him. I don't like this side of me. I miss the old me. Oh, but why am I raging? This emotional sea which stirs in me now, in the new Saul. If not an improvement, an evolution to remain fit in my environment. This is Saul's poor excuse for an excuse. Reminds me of a movie.

There's my prey, ten yards from where I initially shot him, crawling as quickly as he can, while all his brothers run for their lives leaving him on the battlefield. A shame that honor leaves our minds when our flesh beckons for it. The animal seems to always win out over the God. I pull out my knife; he's roughly *fifty yards away*.

I never clean the knife, it carries with it the blood of all my trespassers, all the cowards who tried to kill me and failed. *Twenty-five yards*. He fails to see or hear me, for it is too loud from my men killing his men. *Fifteen yards*. I suddenly see two men running down the hillside raising their guns at me. Damn! It's too late. Pulling up my gun and closing my eyes, I attempt to pull the trigger and hear two shots before mine that don't hit me. Thank you brother, I don't miss a beat, still running. My heart is beating so hard that I feel that flowing river in my ears. *Five yards* and I can see a blood trail from his wound, following him. Everything slows down again. I follow the blood up to his body. In art this would be called an implied line. It is only a line because it generates space in one direction far more than in any other, and its hue is a contrast to its surroundings.

Look how many "it's" that something like a *line* can have. Look what that one little line owns; its hue, its surroundings. Imagine what you could own... Think about it.

Two yards. I scream my loudest scream as he turns and screams as well, firing off two shots in the process; one bounces off my shield, one passing by me. I jump the rest of the way and land in his lap, burying my knife deep in his heart. Right where I said I would.

We pass through this life like a blur
It is this we can concur
Now in my head your spirit stirs
Your body lives everywhere
As it were.

"Hoorah! Booyah! Hoorah! Booyah!" My soldiers holler all over the mountainside, and the words have a weird quality to them. The bellowing lifts up and down like a wave crashing against my ears, with a vacuum of silence between each word that almost feels like air being sucked away from me, and then my ears are fed again with the auditory nourishment, that eases my soul. It is the chant we always yell, when all is well. All the while I am still lying on my victim. Looking at him, hearing the chant in the background gives me an eerie feeling about completing this mission. My victim is not dead yet, and not just that, he is smiling as he opens his blood filled mouth. He says after coughing a bit, "I missed you for you, good luck brother." Those are his last words, with a smile on his face and fading eyes. "What?" I say out loud. That was weird. Why did he say that? "Are we still reckless?" My brother says, checking my mental pulse. I open my eyes. "No, we're done." I say as I stand up and start to turn saying, "But you had better have your shield up because one of those bullets was for you." Sure enough, it was up, which lifted my confused spirits a bit and grounded my heightened state. I walk over to him and hug him. I grab his radio off of his chest and give it to him. "Call it in brother!" I say, and he smiles and calls it in. "Mission One complete!"

END OF MISSION 1

MISSION 2

ALPHA: GEN. SAUL RIVERS REPORTING...

I kneel back-down staring at my victim. I'm still quite flabbergasted by what he said and did, though most of all, what he had done. Why the hell was he smiling? What was he thinking about that was so overpowering a thought; that it would overshadow the power of fear over imminent death?

Maybe he saw God... I take one of his dog tags and leave him with the other. I look at my brother. He is more or less bragging, while explaining his exciting venture and the two men he took out that had the drop on me. "Brother, get me Williamson please?" I ask kindly, feeling in debt to him. "Okay" he says with a serene smile. He takes a few steps back, and radios my lead medic as he heads down the hill.

I take a deep breath while putting a notch in my blade, marking another kill with a little cut of diamond from a ring I almost gave someone. I'm running out of room. It's almost time... I take another deep breath. It takes a lot out of me writing this story. Every skirmish we fight is so demanding. It's exciting and therapeutic for the dark side of me, though it leaves my heart restless. All those dead men, all the bullets, all the blood, and all the heart wrenching screams heard by my partial ears from the mouths of grown men. Men crying like new born babies, wishing they were babies once again being held by their loving mothers. So warm in that crib, maybe being rocked to sleep, being sung a soft song. The author of one of my favorite books, *The Forever War*, said something about the likeness of birth to death. "Both are a bloody mess." I add that they both cry of their misfortune. Though both must be ignorant of their circumstances, one entering the world—one leaving it.

I think the killing may bother me for the most part because I don't get to be intimate with them. This man here beside me is easy. I got to see him face-to-face. He knows me and I know him. He struck me, and I struck him. It's Karma, the balance. Living on this planet, spinning through the universe, is emulated by emotion which spins through our hearts, our minds, and delivers to us an example of equilibrium. No justice, no injustice, just us. Just actions without words, without standards. Everything else kills, everything else eats. Everything else is naked, sleeping with nature. We make things good and bad, measuring action, trying to balance the force. While the rest of the universe remains in a state of balance, we do everything but. Maybe that is why he was smiling. Maybe it all makes sense seconds from death. Those last seconds free us from the confines, the borders we set up for human existence. Liberation in death. Maybe in the state he is in now, he can see that death is quite wonderful. Heart rates up, intensity, anticipation, the chase, fire, lead and fear. These are the colors. This moment with him and I begins to define the canvas' future; Him, dead to the world, me dying a little inside on this mountaintop. That is the final painting, his final strokes on earthy canvas. Those strokes are his final statement in this life echoing the sounds of an era of the fall of man. And I am the lonely art critic, desperately wanting to create "art" of my own. Though instead of this paintbrush, I hold a gun in my hand. The irony is the reality of it.

The Painter

That he is the painter, the painter with one color on his
palette. A sword and a mallet. One bad taste left in his
mouth when he's done painting, he's waiting.
The picture could be a rose petal, or a bit of bright red sunset, but yet.
He knows it to be something vile, unnatural and ugly to the eyes of many.
The painter's heart is heavy.

"Sir!"

Williamson says, calling for my attention.

"SitRep?" I ask.

"Four dead, eight wounded, fifteen M.I.A."

I can see my brother writhing in anger.

"The Four dead, who were they?"

"Four immigrant fighters from Canada."

"The wounded, how bad?"

"None critical sir, patch ups really. As for the Union group, well they're definitely out of pocket. All intelligence gathered points to you. It was a plot to kill you as far as I'm concerned."

"Okay good, the M.I.A. will be radioed, no response than we keep on moving. We will worry about the implications of the Union mission later. Mission Two starts now"

"And what about the four dead men on your hands?!" My brother says with a revolting boldness. I look at Williamson. "Will you give us a minute?" He leaves without a word. As he leaves, I place my gun under my chin, take the safety off and put my finger on the trigger. I speak loud and clear as I ask "What if I pulled this trigger right now and blew my brains out? What would be your next move?" He says nothing and so I elaborate. "As acting colonel directly under my command, you become the leader. So what the bloody hell do you do next?" It is then he opens his fat, sarcastic mouth. "I would purchase a time machine and kill you sooner so that we would have used the incendiary rounds." he says with a shaking emotion in his voice, walking towards me as he speaks, then walking away turning his back to me. He stares over the mountainside very proud of himself, probably feeling liberated from within. I spoil his victory and speak "Okay smarty pants, after you set fire to the mountainside and forced all those armed men down the mountainside towards us, how many of your men would have died then?"

"You're only saying that in hindsight, you were worried about your precious little trees on your stupid bloody hills! So worried about your retarded log cabin from the future we'll never get to see because of your actions! You're selfish!"

"Hindsight or not I was right and you're out of line soldier! Your need to kill over thinking logically troubles me. Sodding flame cans! Shut up about the flame cans and trust me!"

"I'll trust you when you start making sense. And my killing problem? What about you with your going reckless, hunting human beings down like animals? It's an obsession."

"I have set parameters, I'm careful—and that doesn't matter, I have problems and I know it. You on the other hand have an opportunity to be better than me!" I pause and wait a second as some anger boils inside me and I realize I'm not done. Like when you've been puking for a while and try to move away from a dirty toilet. "It's not easy being me you know! This isn't me, this was never me. I do this for you and me to live to see a day we don't have to do this! Pardon me for looking forward to not having to murder people! You're so proud of this way of life like you're getting achievement points on a video game. News flash! This is real life and real people whose lives you ruin!—Does that ever sink into your heart Jacob?!"

I feel better after that, but have not achieved what I set out to in this conversation, so I continue. "You have me to tell you how to be better, to show you how to be the right kind of critic for your big brother and commander. You have me to tell you when *you're* screwing up. You have this beautiful opportunity to learn things ten years before I got to. Don't disrespect your elders' son, let your ego go and revel in a wise man's words so the wise men can revel in yours." I stop and he says nothing. I give him a decent wop on the helmet and say: "You're screwin up!"

I take back my radio from him and order the troops to meet at the top of the mountain underneath the windmills for a briefing. Okay!… it's a hill...a big hill...

MISSION 2

Bravo: Jacob Rivers Reporting...

I probably messed up back they're saying that. I know it wasn't his fault. It was my fault for following him instead of bringing up the rear. Or maybe it was nobody's fault because death happens. Although I don't regret questioning him, it keeps him on his toes. Even if I'm wrong he still ends up doing right by all of us because of the pressure I put on him. I feel like, if he feels he has someone looking up to him, someone he has to impress, that he'll try that much harder to do right. Sometimes I just wish he was more like me. A little more *brutal...*

I'm making my way up the hill, trying to see where he was coming from with all that tree hugger talk. I can't do it. All I see is a squirrel climbing up a tree. When I watch him, Saul, watching things—it's weird. He looks like he is witnessing something so magnificent taking place. Like the Aurora Borealis or an avalanche. He sees something more. He's out of his mind. He's crazy. Who cares about this 'Mother Nature' nonsense! What is he a hippie or something? God, and this going reckless? Really? He can viciously murder one man, but can't efficiently kill a couple hundred? My brother the labyrinth. The only thing that makes me that happy when it appears to me is a woman, and mine was in California. So I destroy everything; I destroy trees and squirrels and soldiers all day with flaming mortar rounds until I see her.

I shake my head in an obvious way, though I must look strange to everyone else considering no one has said anything for quite a while. Though thinking and talking to myself has become a pleasant epidemic of the mind. I make my way to the top of the hill. My brother is standing center stage. Troops are scattered under the trees and in the branches, sitting in them and hanging from them like monkeys, laughing and smiling like children. Throwing poop at each other. That last part isn't true, but I wish it was, what a nice laugh that would be. We do all of this so serenely, laughing and smiling, acting like we all just didn't tap on death's door. Letting apathy reign supreme while we dwell in homes built for empathy. Just like sociopaths.

Anyway, they need to be in the trees because there is no room on the ground. It becomes very difficult to have group therapy with Dr. Rivers when there are 4000 of us in the foothills of Nowhereland. I focus on my brother who's is waving his hands almost frantically. He seems to be in a rush, must not be safe. "Everybody listen up!" I yell to the men who can't hear and or see my brother. It quiets down. I think we're about to become privy to Mission Two.

"I want to talk a little bit about what we're doing. What the missions are and what I expect from everyone" My brother speaks and continues.

"We are simply accomplishing a goal that we've already been shooting for, for years. The difference now is that there is a clock ticking against us. This clock is ticking down to two years from now. This puts a rush on conquest. Therefore, the game changes to all-out war. I said several times before why it never was going to be like this. Diplomacy is extremely effective for peace and efficient on cost to us. Not to mention, *it is our duty as free thinkers to utilize peace.* Though diplomacy will not save this country in two years. With those things considered the game becomes aggressive, alarming, and inhumane. All of you…" He takes a deep breath, pauses, with solemn looks in his eyes, like he just let something go, something he loved that he wasn't sure would return. "… All my men have waited for the day I stopped caring like a humanitarian and starting acting like a soldier one hundred percent. But I will warn you—you do not know me as well as you might think you do and you do not know what I am capable of. You will be so disgusted by my behavior. You will wonder how I can sleep at night. This may sound ridiculous coming from me. But you will see very soon. So I warn you now. The bright side of this fact is you will be on the winning side... You asked me to be a soldier, now you will be terrified of what that truly means." He pauses again and takes a deep breath and releases with profound physicality. "I just want you to know that I love all of you very much, and would do anything for you. I hope that you can stomach my existence when this is all over." He finishes this warning with red eyes and heavy breaths that make his chest look so massive on his otherwise medium built frame.

"These missions are a representation of the physical and mental stress that we will impose upon our enemies. It will be supreme anguish for them. It will viciously navigate through their lives in a swift and appalling matter. So appalling, the anger in their hearts will boil over in a rapid fashion of which they will not be able to control. They will behave recklessly, without regard to themselves or others. As all humans do in the end, they will gather whatever little left they have that represent there flags and facilitate a final attempt to consume us. It is then, we will consume them! With a force they can't imagine... This is how it will end for all who oppose us. This is how our story begins, as the forefathers of a new and glorious nation of enlightenment, passion, and strength. I expect from you all, everything that you can possibly give me. Both sweat and sorrow, sacrifice and protection. With no questions about the Missions or my intentions. It's not safe for anyone to know, I ask you to trust me with everything in you because I have never forsaken you." My brother pauses with a steely look in his eyes. Like he was looking down the barrel of some kind of pain, seeing how ugly it would get, but knowing how necessary it would be. I wish you could see his face. The definition of bittersweet, "Is that understood?!" my brother bellows out to the confused crowd. "YES SIR!" I scream without a doubt in my mind that everyone said it with me, even if they were completely bewildered. My brother smiles and says: "Good, because our next move is to get down through this valley northward for roughly four miles to a large convoy of supply trucks with a capacity of 500 soldiers. We will pack in those five hundred soldiers and ship them out." This is a statement deserving of questions, and while I wait for somebody to speak up, no one does, and no questions are asked. This is my brother's legacy.

"We need to take this mission very seriously. We need to take it seriously because the Crimson Army call this territory their home. We all know they've had the choke for quite some time so it is no surprise that they would have a camp here. We also know how pissed they are at us for royally disrupting there style and sending Osiris to hell!" Many men laugh, some cheer with me. My brother just smiles, giving everybody the roughneck they want, holding back the peaceful savior in him we would reject. I hate the Crimson so bad. It's their fault *they're* gone. What's worse is they don't care, even after how close my brother and Adis were. Even after the blade. It was Luther's fault this all went to the dogs; it was his fault there was even a war to begin with. His fault I've been an adult since I was a kid. My brother walks to the edge of his little pedestal pointing at some of the men in front and continues. "So you had better bet your hides they're defending it." He pauses, "We are going to avoid engaging the enemy as we have been," boos and awes are heard from the crowd. My brother smiles and laughs, "Have you not had enough combat today?!" Some no's, nevers and laughter from the crowd. "Have you not had your share of blood for the season?!" More commotion from the crowd. "Alright! enough fooling around, we're going to make a quick stop along the way to tie up a loose end and then we're off to the highway, to the trucks. Am I understood?! Are my men ready?!" "Sir Yes Sir!" We all say with excitement. We say it like it's one word Siryessir! Like it has its own meaning, each segment losing its individual purpose to become something greater and all the while uglier. An impending destructive force. An answer to a question of something summing to war, or simply death and destruction to be modest.

My brother jumps off his earthy soapbox and walks down the mountainside. We all move into whatever formation we can and follow behind at once. This is my brother's legacy. As I am behind my brother working into his peripherals there is a subtle physical recognition of his awareness to me. "Jacob." He says softly. "Yea" I say as I speed up to make eye contact. "I need you to do me a favor." Here it comes. I knew I wouldn't be getting off that easy. "I need you to bury our friend the sniper." He puts out three fingers, saturates my view with them and says "three feet deep." "Yes sir." I say and salute in a matter not to be confused with sarcasm, and make my way back to the body. Three feet isn't so bad. The amount of feet I had to dig was based solely on the degree of my insubordination, so it's not too bad. I got six feet once when I pulled a gun on him, he said because I behaved like a dog, I should dig it deep enough so that fellow canines couldn't uncover and spoil my work. For that would make me look bad among the canine community. I dug it with my paws, like a dog... With no shortage of bodies to bury, he always had a 'corner' to put me in. My brother told me while I dug that six foot hole with my bare hands that if he didn't love me so much he would have killed me with his. That just reminded me, I forgot about father's day. Forgot to wish him a happy one...

MISSION 2

CHARLIE: GEN. SAUL RIVERS REPORTING...

He's right, and he's wrong. I got down off my heap of high ground and sent him on his way to be punished for being wrong and right simultaneously. I start walking with my men, feeling a strange aching in my stomach. Strange but familiar. I turn around and tell one of my captains to take the lead of the pack down to the stream at the bottom of the hillside. I walk back to my sniper friend and his underpaid undertaker. I take it slow going back because I want to have the right words for him. The speech I just gave was for my troops. The speech I just gave was not for my little brother. He deserved much more. God bless him, he didn't need it from me. He didn't ever need much besides answers to questions. Good questions, with answers I did not have. Questions about life, about men dying. As if living was logical and dying was unnecessary. Imagine telling a child why men screamed for their mothers before they died in the middle of an active battlefield. Imagine having to stop what I was doing so he would pick his gun back up and continue doing what he didn't understand. Explaining why blood pours out of a man's mouth, while he shakes before death. Sometimes at night we would go to a fantasy world, where men die and go to a beautiful place where war is only an old story, and pretty girls and steak dinners were never in short supply. We went to this place on every night that we had a rough day. It became a reality for him. But I knew this wasn't true. Not here in this place. That place where everything feels right and no one dies is where God lives. But God doesn't live here. He didn't build this house for himself, he built it for us. I could never tell him why this was the way things were, I just knew it was. That was never good enough for him. That is why he digs the sniper's grave. Because I am not God. I am just a piece of him. A piece that has lost his way.

Despite the arguments, but God, not counting them, he followed me blindly; this is a good thing in war, when your leader has his head on straight… From all accounts my 'axis' is only slightly tipped, like the earth. So like earth I had seasons governed by the events and people in my life. Sometimes I am cold when the times provoke me, like a winter storm. Sometimes I am mild and forgiving even nourishing, like a spring rain. Because of this seemingly logical character I display the blind loyalty makes sense. This blindness he has for me was good in every situation we have encountered thus far. Though now, the way things have changed... You see I can't quite explain the terrible things that I will begin to do. I can't justify it in any way in my head other than the way the Department of Defense had often justified war. Coldly with a matter of fact feeling with a background of righteous justification, "We're better than them." and "All is fair in love and war." come to mind. "Terrorism!" is one of my favorites though. So I learn from my four fathers to tell a lie, a terrible lie. Reminds me of a song.

For now it's whatever works, because his natural blindness would not be enough. He would have to be very blind, so blind that I would have to help him. What I am about to do, what these next few missions will do, will be morally devastating. So ethically questionable that the Devil himself might have something to say. I see him digging. I clear my throat to gain his attention. He looks up and smiles awkwardly. "Hey." I say: "Hey yourself." he says with a smile.

"Look—"

"Don't say it, you were right, and I was wrong." He puts up a hand in surrender. He means well when he cuts me off. He's a little bastard, but he's my little bastard now, and he's doing alright. Little things like that rebuild my hope in this reincarnated Alexander the Great. "I forgot about Father's day brother." "It's been months, I'm not worried, I'm sure we were busy being shot at or something."

"Either way, Happy Father's Day brother."

I sit and think about it for a minute. I feel like he's giving me a guilt trip.

Quickly, I realize the guilt is internal. "Thank you." I say and add "As a gift I would ask if you would allow me to dig this hole with you."

"Alright, but only 'cuz I owe ya one." he smiles and shakes his head sarcastically, "I won't let you off so easy tomorrow." I laugh, pull out my combat shovel and start digging.

It's really quiet for the first foot and a half, still searching for those words. The *hole* thing is so symbolic. We're both stuck in *this* together, trying to gather our thoughts; gather our wits, trying to keep them about us. We're in it even though we don't have to be, only because we think we should be. Ironically, all we do is dig ourselves deeper. There's something special about this hole though. It makes us very much alike. Our common ground is the fact that very soon we would be burying many bodies in the soil. I would be more like him soon. More like him, than he is. I believe he will begin to take on my role as the peacemaker. Trying to balance the mobile of this life he perceives. He thinks "Someone's got to do it right?" Someone's got to be the bad guy, make the tough choices; someone's got to do the *right* things too. And they have to fight with each other because their belief systems are different right? And it all makes sense and so it feels safe. We create a matrix, a myriad of ideals, pigeon holding ourselves into the pluming fires of good and evil. The truth is we are ever in a state of danger, safety is the constant illusion. Conflict and resolution is the true state of existence that we so often misinterpret. We only desire comfort and simplicity because we can't have it. We're ever longing for something that gets farther and farther away from us as life complicates, proliferates in constant progression.

I know my brother; he will do anything to feel safe again. Something he hasn't felt in years, like that Sunday dinner... He will finally see what death does to me because he will finally see what it's doing to him…

I feel like death takes a little piece of you. Every time you do it, every time you see it. Every time it makes you cry or wonder why, it's burnt in there somewhere screaming your name. In my case it screams in anger if I killed them, and sometimes it screams with a sorrow rooted in helplessness because I let them die. He will now feel that feeling and he will be shocked; he will be sickened by me. I get a stomach ache thinking about it. So be it, damned to hell. The words are there suddenly. Here it goes. "I know what you mean by maybe making a bad call back there. I understand where you're coming from… With that being said I am sorry you feel that way. I'm sorry because the decision I made was a great decision. You don't see this because you don't have all the pieces and so you can't see the end result." He looks at me with a passing intensity. "You can't add up the equation. I've kept several numbers and variables away from you, and for good reason. If you have patience with me it will pay off, and I promise when Mission Two is complete you will understand better." I pause and let this sink in. I say as seriously as I can "I'm going to ask you to do something when Mission Two is complete, something very important. I need you by my side completely in order to do it. I hope you can understand this without needing an explanation because I need you to do something now as well. I need you to trust me completely without criticism. Some of my decisions will seem terrible and audacious...I need you to be terrible and audacious with me. I need you to have faith in the notion that everything I do is in the best interest of you, me and the entire team. Everything we care about has been in consideration with these missions. I promise that you will be completely satisfied in the end."

We dig the rest of the hole without a word. He's thinking very hard. I can feel it. He's doesn't appease. He isn't going to tell me what I want to hear; only what *he* wants to do. I get up out of the hole as he does. We take one last look at our friend and kick him into his new home. We bury him in the side of this mountain. "Peace be with you." I say. My brother puts a hand on my shoulder and cracks a smile. That kind of smile you might find on a soldier who's done some stuff he ain't proud of, thinking he shouldn't be smiling, like some sucker that thinks the world is peachy. It feels real when it's not so perfect. Feels like something human.

He says: "I got your back, I always will." A weight is lifted off of my shoulders, as a new one begins to rest, heavier than the first. It's times like these I realize I am not okay. No matter what, something keeps the burners on, even when there isn't anything to burn. When there is something worth keeping me in turmoil, it feels good. It feels like home. My soul seems to be performing constant triage on my mind, on the pain, This is probably a good place for a soldier anyway. Stuck on something that becomes a driving force, hoping one day, things would go back to the day before, though ready when it doesn't. I know I really just need to let go…But, I swear I won't, not until it's over. Not until I'm sure. My brother and I walk down to the bottom of the mountain with the rest of the troops who are wading in the river. It's going to be hard for a few days ahead, on me and my people. I stop thinking about the missions for a minute, and stare out. I try to forget everything that has happened. Forget about war and blood and death. Forget about what had happened to my mother and sister. My best friend and the love of my life, I forget they were all taken away from me. For a heartbeat, for one breath, and then another, and another. I forget about houses and television and video games. Republicans and Democrats, hatred and racism, until everything is gone. I look at these bright greens. It's not a fern, it's just something alive and beautiful that arises from the earth and gives me something to take in. Nourishment for my lungs, some kind of pleasantry for my eyes. Every leaf is like the whole of the plant. A beautiful repetition, an ode to the entire being is found in every component of itself. Repercussion; like sound waves of thunder playing back for everyone within earshot. The stream is like a void of untouchable mystery, it has a glassy, metallic look to it. The current is strong and the sun shines through the trees. Closer observation yields more truth about the shiny beast, but I forget that it's water. I let it be whatever it is without me, without labels given by the strange upright things that commit terrible deeds and still live most righteous on the earth. I let it ride over my mind like the water would ride over my body. I take a deep breath, and I let it be…

Take a break.
Take a breath.

Remember being a child...
With less words...
With less pain...
Take a breath.

Take a break.
I'll do the same.

I begin to think very hard about the next few hours, the next few days in effect to Mission Two. I start to think about where we are going right now. Do you remember when I said that the enemy over the hill was terrifying? I wasn't talking about those Union girls we just tap danced all over. I was talking about what we are about to come in close contact with. The enemy we never fight, unless we absolutely have to. It is fortunate that the Union Army is dumb enough to fight them for us. So they splash and splash and erode the rock a bit.

It is what the Crimson do that makes me avoid them. It's what they did to me. It's about pain and mental distress. That's why I knew they didn't shoot at me earlier. They like to be real close when their victim dies. Oh the writhing. Oh the begging. The hot breath pouring out with the blood on a cool, misty day. The worthless opponent contorting like a dying snake. They take it in. It completes the kill.

I need to destroy them and do what I set out to do and kill their leader. I want him dead; I want all of them dead, save two. This is a group that my best friend helps lead. The group of people the love of my life left me for. Besides igniting a fire of rage in me I can't bare or bare to explain, it does something else. It scares me, they scare me. The voice of this group does not speak words, it simply is. It is a concept, a notion, an idea. It's everything I ever tried to do my way, but it worked their way. It is a practice, a way of life. It is so powerful, that despite my charisma, despite my knowledge and communication skills, despite the fact that these two people were the most important people in my life, it swept them away, in an instant. Like a red flood. Rich in spirituality, intelligence, and an understanding of deep knowledge, of things I can't even fathom to be true. They make it true. I feel so worthless. I feel so inadequate that it has become real physical pain. When I speak of them in disgust, it is only because I am distressed and in disgust with myself. If anyone else hates them it is because they do not understand them. I pretend to hate them because it makes me feel good. What do they say? Feeds the ego? I almost convince myself of the hate. But, they are a great and passionate people. They are beautiful and intense. As is *she*. They accomplish things in this physical world that people can only dream of, literally. Jacob was in a coma for a week because one of the Crimson masters touched him.

They're like vampires. They can steal your energy and feed it to themselves, to each other. It's amazing and I didn't believe it myself until it happened to me. I watched my energy go into them, they shared it and fed off of it. I could see it, the *ether,* the *Murrock,* but only for a moment, the light, the colors, it was so beautiful, and then it was gone. I believe they see the way I saw, except they see it all the time. And they can feel you coming. They're not great at gun slinging, that's us. But they don't appear to care or to need such traits. They're plugged into something great. Their leader though? Luther? He is the Devil on earth. He does not deserve his throne. They worship him, it's sick really. I want to gouge my eyes out when I see his face... He killed my mother and my sister. He is responsible for this bloody, vicious war. And he will pay with his blood, by the dagger he gave me years before. How did he discover the *Murrock?* Why was he chosen?

With that being said, they are a supreme opponent who have developed a completely new and devastating way of waging war. One day you will understand better, but not today.

We make it downstream a bit and I call for a break for everyone, save a couple hundred spotters. I give enough time for the spotters to switch out. I sit down and fill my canteen. I have to make another speech. This is one of coercion and convincing. I think back to one of my professors in college who taught me persuasive speaking. The do's and do not's of wooing your crowd into submission; I wonder what he would tell me now. What words of wisdom would he have for me? Maybe he could tell me how to convince my people to fight the force I had forced them to avoid like the plague. Sure they wanted to fight them, they were more than ready. But they knew I wasn't, and that would trouble them, my one eighty all of a sudden. They weren't dummies. I don't know for sure what my professor would say, but knowing him, he would probably say something ridiculously sarcastic like "It's not like your convincing them to kill women and children!" I didn't even have to tell them it was Crimson. I could say they were crack troops from the Union. They knew we were about to tread in Crimson territory, but they also knew Union was dumb enough to squat here. I could lie, they would believe whatever it was that I said. No matter what, they would consider it a reasonable order. By the time they realized what was going on it would be too late. Lying would change things though. I would lose something very important from them. I wonder how I'd get it back.

"Alright everyone!" I yell to my troops. "About three and a half miles due east is a Union army fortress that was set up a few months back as a 'seek and destroy' operation for the eastern chapter of our army; essentially us. Mission Two is to destroy the fortress and all of its inhabitants, salvaging what we can for supplies. We only need a team of about one hundred soldiers, so I will need all Alpha and Bravo Captains and Lieutenants to select their five best men and join me and Colonel Rivers down through the stream and up through a mountain pass eastward. As we come down past the summit, the fortress will become visible. At which point we will surround the compound and kill the fifteen sentries in place. This is phase one. Once phase one is complete we will initiate phase two. Heavy artillery and invasion no prisoners, no survivors, period." I wait for a moment to hear any questions.

"Since you're still honoring my policy of don't ask don't tell, I will tell you. We have an American U.A.V. at our disposal, given to us by our friend. It's American made, the Union has been duped into thinking it is theirs. It has been very helpful with logistics and planning in consideration of this mission. In the future, it will be helpful as we head into the end of this war. It doesn't seem like much, but we've moved mountains with less." They never question who my friend is anymore. They didn't question much at all even before I had asked them not to. They would know my friend soon. They would have to know them. It was their friend as much as it was mine. I speak up again, "We leave in five, all men involved in the skirmish report a quarter mile down the stream. All other soldiers please sit by the stream and enjoy the view. That's an order. We will radio to you when we are done or if there is a need for reinforcements." As the Captains start picking out their best, my brother joins me as I start walking downstream.It's quiet for a minute, until he asks, "So who is your friend, brother? I find that he is more and more influential as time proceeds. He was almost non-existent a month ago. What kind of alliance have you made and with whom? Is it Crimson again?"

"God no!"

"Then who is it, pardon my persistence, but I believe I have the right to know."

"You have every right to know, but I don't have to tell you." There is a pause as a result of confusion. My brother, with a bewildered look in his face, replies, "So what does that mean?"

"It means you will be meeting him soon, or them I should say. You are going to parlay with our friend and pick up a few things." He looks surprised with a taste of nervousness. I knew what he was thinking, some mysterious entity that only I was in contact with that he knew nothing about suddenly showing up to him? Why was he going before he knew what it was? We're dealing with weapons and war and such, so there is an element of danger there.

Regardless of the fact that I was his brother and I would never put him in a position to be hurt in any way, it was still a bit unnerving I'm sure. And, regardless of his fervor a moment ago, no one really wants to see the cow die, they just want that delicious, guilt free cheeseburger at the end. So now my brother is a bit flabbergasted. He doesn't know what to say. He probably doesn't care to know the identity of the friend anymore. It has probably become the farthest thing from his mind already. He doesn't even take the time to ask the logical questions, like when, where, how. He will get there soon I hope. I need him to be a leader as much as I am one. I don't know what tomorrow holds for my body, or my mind. I need to know he can take the reins. I hope *Mission Three* will help him with that.

The five minutes it takes for my troops to make it over the pass goes by quick, because it's coming. I didn't want it to go by at all. I'd rather be stuck in this moment forever. Though there is nothing particularly great about this moment, there is something particular that lies ahead. It is an event horizon for these missions. It is the domino effect, the no turning back point. Once I start this fire it will not go out until the end, until there is no one left except one group with one mentality. I can still turn back right now, disband all of my troops and head into the Adirondacks, like we all did when the war started. But, for what? To wait for commies and blokes to move in and make it theirs? That won't happen. I may be a "traitor" to my country, but **I** believe I am a true American. Whatever that word still means, that is who I am, and how I will die, if I must. The hundred or so people suit up and go hot as I inform them to. We make our way down the stream and keep a good foot speed. A quick jog maybe eight miles an hour. That makes it about a thirty minute trek. I'm calculating this because of the fear and anticipation I feel in the strongest way I have since the beginning of the war.

When the Crimsons attacked the capital, nothing could stop them. They had all the supplies they needed, impeccable discipline and military training. They had something else too, some kind of unstoppable feeling. An unshakable chill that they ran up the spines of their enemies, like a flag pole, raising their red flag of doom. Something special and terrifying, it was a way about them that was mysterious and ominous. Their minds, and their abilities to falter the minds of others, was their ultimate weapon. They have done things to me, in my mind that defies rational thought. They appear to be irrational. This is their intention. It confounds their enemy and depresses them, suppresses them. It hurts so bad when a people so emotionally mature can cause so much pain and not care. Yet every facet of their existence is rich with emotion.

It's like they're aliens from another world who understand us, empathize with us, only so they can wreak havoc on us. They tear apart our souls. They bring out the emotional baby in us and then spank it.I wrote a poem about them. How they made me feel after an ambush in Pennsylvania a couple of months back. I was in so much pain. The sorrow I had at this time was unbearable. Writing for me brings me a peace that screaming and killing can't. It's the escape with resolution. I needed it to go away. This poem dulled those feelings a bit.

Sometimes

Sometimes they use arrows that cut through our bone marrow
Sometimes they're big, and kill us instantly
Sometimes they're small, wounding soldiers, making
them more trouble than they're worth
More trouble than their birth
Sometimes they go right through their spines... Sometimes
Sometimes they don't hit the spines because they're soaked with poison
Sometimes the poison waits and creeps
Sometimes hours, days, or weeks
Sometimes it's contagious, mortifying, the pain's outrageous
I'm outraged it's
Something that leaves me faithless
When you only know these men you're with, the arrows are black plague
Sometimes they use bullets, sometimes their rusty blades
They show my men the face,
of death so close that if they live they'll never be the same
Sometimes those men kill themselves...
Sometimes I am angry and I scream out in rage for my offenders!

Sometimes I cry for my men
Sometimes I sob with pity for the human race
And after all these things, sometimes I wish for death
The one that takes the longest

They do these things, not because they are sick, but because they understand what it is to be sick. They are good people somewhere deep down inside. Like me. I think we are all good people in a bad thing called war. He would say: "It doesn't matter how it's done, or who else dies, and it doesn't matter how they die. This is a trivial thing...All that matters is that you...and me are standing here, still breathing. In the end, it all vanishes..." This is their leader, Luther. The son of a bitch that made this happen, the one who killed my family. Why me!? He's a maniac! Bless his people, they are a great people ill-advised by a lunatic who seems to be obsessed with me, yet disposes of all around me regardless of my ties! My best friend is one of their generals. He is in way over his head. He understands them to a point, but he is not one of them. Back then my friend, Adis, just wanted to see the world burn, and the Crimson just happened to be having a bonfire. It all happened when the *Community* split into two factions. The Crimsons as they were eventually known, took a liking to Luther and Adis' style. The rest of the peaceful, sane individuals stayed with me. It was my baby, the Community, and it had a brother out of nowhere that mutated. Insane people started crawling out of crevices in every direction. It was turmoil and chaos. Then, Luther, who was just as crazy as them, took the reins and tamed them. Made a single and concise, cerebral entity now known as the Crimson army. How could a man so unscrupulous, so outrageous and unhinged make it work? I don't know, but the Crimsons grew and flourished. The mass of maniacs calmed and became structured. We allied with them and ripped apart the American Army together. And I had my best friend back for a while, though I was lying to myself. I was only trying to get close to Luther, so I could kill him. Reminds me of a movie.

It was about Adis, it was about Luther, it was about her. But I don't want to talk about her right now…

I choked, I lost it and I killed Osiris and half of his regiment. It felt good to satisfy the anger, but it wasn't enough. I needed Luther. I still need him! I need him dead. I need my blade twisting in his torso somewhere. Where it hurts the most. I have asked men how badly it hurts when I stab them, so that I would know such a thing. I would twist the blade and whoever I was killing, would become Luther. I would stare at him and listen to him bellow. Listen for the anguish in the rarest, most terrible form. That's how I found it. Under the ribs weaving in and out a few of them at a diagonal upward twisting back and forth. The look of malice and anger in my face would be the last thing he would ever see. "I got you! You son of a-!" My friend thought he was some kind of Napoleon in his own little Golden age. What it really boils down to though, is that he just needed someone to believe in him. He needed a following. Didn't matter who really, it could have been the God forsaken Nazi's as long as they saluted and cheered. I feel that one day I will experience a grand bittersweet, when I destroy the Crimson army. He will be free and he will come with me. She will be free too. I would be validated, because they would be lost without me.

Thirty minutes go by quick, quicker than the five before. We have made it up this mountain of mine. How long did I climb? Reminds me of a song. I clear my throat and speak to my men as once again my Captains reiterate my message. I talk softly and so they do as well. We are very close.

"Attention all troops," I speak and point down toward the valley. "This is where the compound lies. It is a circular structure with 15 sentries placed somewhat evenly around the circumference of dense trees that disguise the fortress. I need my snipers. Thirteen of them staggered in arrangement with a target. Jacob and I will fill up two northwest targets. Surround yourself around the dense trees at the center of the valley. Stay on high ground, slow and quiet. Three minutes... go. Zach, do you have the flame cans and mortars ready?" "Yes sir." he replies. "Assemble the teams up on the edge of that high point to the south." "Yes sir." I address the whole team again, "Everyone on channel five." It takes two and a half minutes and my men are ready. "I get fourteen "Ready sirs." Thirteen snipers and Zack; commanding the mortar team. "Okay has everyone acquired their own target?" "Lock one." One of my Captain communicates "Lock two," "Lock three," In succession to thirteen. "Stay locked, and get your guns hot." I say, as I hail my brother and we walk together to the last two positions. We grab our two targets and we hit fifteen.

"Okay everyone, take it easy and listen carefully. Number one, we will all shoot on a three count given by me. Two—" "Sir!" Someone interrupts me. "They're not Union, their Crimson!" I slight surprise and a bit of terror reins in his voice. "Shut up while I'm talking soldier, they are disguising themselves to divert you. Do not be fooled!" I continue "Secondly after the target is down do not engage anyone or anything else, is that understood?" Tons of scrambled "Sir yes sirs." go over the waves. They sound nervous, they sound like they don't believe me. But they listen just the same. Thank God.

"But sir?!" Another anxious voice over the radio. There's always one right? I respond sharply "Listen to me! Listen very carefully I told you that things would not be as they seemed. I told you, you would have to trust me no matter what, and you promised!" Silence sweeps. Serene Silence fills my soul. The last quiet moment I will experience for a while. Here, it goes. "On three...One, Two, Three!" All at once fifteen shots. All men, confirm their kills. I hope to keep this hold on my troops. Why do they love me and trust me so? I hope I can figure out the formula because right now it appears to be madness. "Sir, there are unknown targets coming from the bush, moving in on downed targets." Another Captain reports over the radio. "Do not engage, report back immediately." I order quickly as to not lose any of *my men*.

I set my radio to channel four and wait. A minute passes "Clear," a mysterious voice from the radio says. I change back to channel five. "All mortar teams fire into the dense forest beyond the sentry perimeter!" The incendiary rounds launch and barrel into the forest. "Phoot, Phoot, Phoot!" to my right the mortar rounds arc over with a perfect, mathematically brilliant climb, apex and descent upon the fortress like a forest. "Boom, Boom!" over and over again. Fire oozes out everywhere like a liquid that catches on the leaves and small branches turning into a beautiful, full, fragrant fire. You can smell that smell so quick—reminds me of a song. Fire rains down upon my enemies. And it burns and burns. I am mesmerized by the flames. I sit and stare at them for quite some time. I imagine that my men are doing the same. I see my troops come around and down the mountain, coming to join me around the campfire. The fire soothes me. You know that cracking sound that wood makes as it breaks down and collapses? The forest makes this sound, but so much louder, with hints of other noises and effects. Like if a man falls from a building, as opposed to a cat. More to tell with the larger entity, more to experience.

The fortress like a forest makes a sound like a deep thunder. A thunderous whooping clap, accompanied, and so proven to exist by the fire, like lightning. The fire claps and waves like an orange flag of my disposition. This sound drowns out the screams of anguish that lie within the compound as my channel four soldiers make sure the doors stay shut. It feels good. But it is also torture. For them and for me. If it was my choice, I wouldn't have it this way. But it wasn't my choice, it was Luther's and Luther's alone...I made a promise to my mother as she died in my arms. I promised her I would do whatever I had to do to keep my brother alive. Any cost, any means. Lives mean nothing to me as they stand next to the supreme value of my brother's. Regardless of my baggage and my hang ups, he comes first. He's all I really have left. He is the only one that hasn't left me for the Crimson or Heaven. And we will see this war through, me and him. All the way to the end, if anyone stands in our way for an instant, it will be in that same instant that they will perish. *Anyone.*

It burns for hours and hours until the night is old and the day is almost born. It is confounding to my soldiers that the fire doesn't spread. That storm comes. The storm my brother predicted this morning. It starts to extinguish the fire, as if it always had a part in the mission. I stand out in the rain, away from the trees, and let it wash over me. Will you wash away my sins? Will you cleanse me? Or will you find that the things I have done bear too much evil? Will you strike me down with fierce lightning? Please kill me now...

Time goes slow now, as my channel four men regroup with the rest of the troops, knowing their job is done. All the other soldiers start to realize they were the missing troops from the Union ambush this morning. My brother sees them and looks at me. He just smiles and shakes his head. Thinking about the flame cans and the missing soldiers. It all makes sense now, huh baby brother? I laugh out loud a bit and he sees it and chuckles, putting two thumbs up. He may fight tooth and nail with me, thinking I'm crazy in my decision making, though I always seemed to surprise him in the end. One of my channel four boys walks up to me, looking confused and sick to his stomach he hands me a key and says: "I heard the screams." I say: "I know, and I am sorry for that. I am sorry I made you responsible." It's Chris, and Chris understands. You will understand Chris much more in the future. You will understand why I chose Chris to lead the channel four men. Regardless of his strength, he looks like he wants to die. He should. He knows what I know. I know I want to die a little bit.

It is time. It is time to call in Mission Two. I walk down to the edge of the fortress like a forest and place myself right in front of a door like a tree trunk. I stare at the keyhole like a slit in the bark. I look at the key and flip it a couple of times in my hand. My heart beats faster. God it's so fast. My body throbs with a sick anticipation. I take the key and put it into the keyhole like a slit in the bark. The door that looks like a tree trunk opens slowly and a burst of hot air hits us smelling of carbon and burning flesh. I walk in first and see exactly as I expected. There are many dead bodies; against the walls of the fortress, hanging out of small buildings in open areas holding small things in their arms. There are claw marks on the walls of the fortress that tells of sounds and sights I can only hear and see in my mind. I stop looking at the bodies. I don't care to look at them, I know what they are. I wonder if maybe my men wouldn't look so closely. I wonder if anyone will be lucky enough that they don't realize. It is far too much to hope for, I quickly hear it. Those gasps for air like the air just isn't enough. That resonant moaning with a tone of instant guilt and feeling of dirty, they are helpless in their need to cry out to me. "Sir we made a mistake! These are just women and children! Crimson women and children!" What a great soldier, putting my weight on his back.

Here we are at my event horizon. My world is now a much different shade of gray. It's more like black now. I take a deep breath and hold it for a moment. I cringe as I push out "There is no mistake... Mission Two complete." The world goes cold and silent again, just as it did when my family lost its women and children. I begin to feel very dizzy. My soldiers realizing what has happen here makes it more real for me. I almost got all the way through without really thinking about it. I almost got to turn my back and play pretend.

The moon is lovely tonight. It's completely full. The clouds from the storm are moving away quite dramatically. It's shaping up to be a decent evening. My men are desperately silent, waiting for something, but I have nothing to give. And they just stay where they are like some confused, but obedient pack of dogs. Even my brother stays off the radar. I imagine the visually incredible still frame I have created behind me as I look at my moon. Just think of all the colors and contrast. The engaging symbolism, think of all the emotion that might be captured in a moment like this. There would be no question as to the meaning of the painting.

I stop looking up for a moment, to look down, where I should be looking. I stare at a particularly beautiful woman that wasn't completely consumed by the fire. She is mostly naked with some of her clothes singed by fire and sticky from her blood. Her last moments were probably torment in her mind and smoke in her lungs. Yet, still she probably had love in her heart. She did not deserve this, but Luther did. And I deserve that gratification. I stare at the ground next to her, and I pretend I am not human for a moment. I pretend I don't know what ground is, that I have never seen it before. I pretend I have never seen the thing they call woman. I then begin to see no difference from the ground and her. I see nothing worth caring for.

So it is now that I ask, what is the root of compassion? When we forget about labels, when we stop looking at things for what they mean or represent, and we just understand how they exist visually in our world, ideals fade to black. All characteristics converge into oneness. It becomes the simple yet all powerful all encompassing *is-ness*. When you do this, my faithful reader, a human being becomes just a splash of paint on the canvas. No different from the field they lie in, the sidewalk they move upon. Their motion means nothing. It does not bring them to life.

With this program of thought initiated I ask a second question. How do I feel about her? When she isn't *her* anymore. When all things of love and caring are forced to disappear, consumed by is-ness. Where smiles don't mean a damned thing. Do we feel nothing? Or do we feel everything all at once? Is compassion an inherent human quality? Or are we taught to care, pretending a civilized world is anything more than an illusion, a dream created by predecessors searching for order and control? When everything is exactly the same, do we feel compassion for all things? Or nothing? Right now, I feel nothing...

This is my legacy now. A cold hearted son of a gun who will stop at nothing to win. To war on nations and factions. To fill my enemies with such anguish that they dream of death. These were all the women, all the loves of the Eastern Division Crimsons. These were also their children, their next generation; in this, the most well conceived, well hidden compound. The most heavily protected in the ways of trickery and illusion. I will find you just the same and I will reign down on you with fire and hate! All is fair in love and war. And in this war there is no you, there is only me. These are my bloody hands. These are *my* Missions.

END OF MISSION 2

"Commander Rivers! Crimson!"

C://Run/Armory/Equipment/MissionOne+MissionTwo

/

/

/

/

/

/

Access Denied

Arrival of the Assassins

The all seeing journalist reports…

October 2nd:

There is no way in the matter of brute force that will destroy the young King Saul, for this is certain. There is a need for a specialized force that will reckon with the mind, body and soul of the Young King. This is understood by the Crimson, and so from overseas to their "friend" they beckon for an answer to the problem that is The Antifederalist Army. This answer comes swiftly in the form of a large plane with roaring engines soaring over Lake Winnipeg in the central region of Canada, just above Minnesota. Though it is important to understand that not even a flying fortress could bring the Young King down, for this would be an apparent attempt of brute force. It is what sits in wait inside this plane that can surely bring the Young King down. These are the men that come from a friend whose techniques, weapons, and sublime genius may be enough to completely destroy the Crimson's enemy through the obliteration of its leader. Two men sit in wait in the cargo area of this plane. These men; One unlike the other, one accenting the other's abilities to the teeth. These are the teeth that fill the jaw of the concept known as "Total Warfare." I peer inside this cargo area of the plane that is soaring thousands of feet in the air and see these assassins. Just two men, silent amidst the dark corridor only lit by a rotating red light that gleams an ominous glare of crimson over our assassins. There is one man who sits across from the other, across from the crimson light, whose physical presence is an intimidating one at the least. He is a large man, well-built, yes, extremely muscular and lean. He carries on his person an array of death machines that would cripple the Young king's stride, had he tried to carry this load. This man they call Super Snake is a death machine himself whose only purpose for eight years has been killing strong men, kings, and Gods among the races. He leans over his own frame, elbows resting on his knees and silently chews on seeds and fruit of varying forms. His armor is beautiful. His armor is unreal, unique in every way. Where vicious, exquisite muscle does not gleam through there are scales upon scales of Kevlar, diamond and platinum.

He drops a seed to the floor of the plane, but swiftly snatches it up from the floor with his thumb and pointer finger. A fluid movement that makes him look less like a human and more like something else. He places the seed on the tip of his tongue, slowly bringing the nourishment within. He stares out a porthole window probably wondering about his prey. He stares with quiet eyes, silent eyes that one peers into and gets lost in instantly. A silence so inviting yet so dangerous. The eyes seem so soft and serene, but the eyes of a wise creature are governed by a will that can make them appear in any way it's master pleases. These eyes may be perceived as soft, but they are so hard from within and filled with ill intent. These eyes represent the power of murder and malice that this creature has to offer to the meek in an unforgiving world. The world that does not forgive, is the habitat built for the Super Snake. The Snake slithers down the benches to the back of the plane as he senses an imminent checkpoint in this mission. He calls over to the man by the red light. This man pulls his eyes from a book he is reading that was written by *a young man in need of a revolution*. He gets up from his seat and walks toward the end of the plane with the Snake. We can now see the parachutes that have always been strapped to their backs, waiting to play their part in the greatest of all missions these two men will ever attempt.

Ten Miles from the Crown Chakra Station, rich foliage grows softly over hard concrete and steel in an otherwise natural setting. Up above, something like a bird soars through the sky. Though it doesn't chirp like a bird, it roars like a lion. As it soars far enough away from the station to avoid suspicion, it releases its precious cargo. Out of the tail of the bird like a lion, two specs fall out, like the *non living excrement that represents the last meal.* Not too far from the truth, as we begin to better see the true nature of these specs. The truth becomes like the earth, as the specs speed toward it at their terminal velocities; getting closer and closer to this truth, not realizing its gravity. I can first see the difference in mass. The Snake is much larger, heavier, denser... He falls at a higher velocity than Sophistico. His ominous nature in the physical realm matches his character. But don't be fooled by

Sophistico. What he lacks in brutality he overshadows with cunning and deceit. I am a reporter, so my job is to report the facts without bias, but I will tell you that the will of these men is evil and without remorse. How are they evil you ask? In a new world where good men do terrible things and bad men claim to be righteous, the duality of good and evil becomes a strange thing. Though some things are constant like the constant of gravity that pulls these men toward the earth, not knowing how its role in nature has played a role in a terrible yet redeeming domino effect that will throw our Saul into kingship, there are constants of good. Love, truth, contemplation of actions and results... are some constants.

These men do not adhere to any such beliefs. The ends always justify the means for these two men no matter the cost of the means, no matter how worthless the ends become. There is no love of their fellow man and the women they could love. No belief in a higher power to humble them in moments of ignorance. For these men, after the bullet passes through their victim's heart, after they wipe their blade clean, it doesn't matter where anyone goes, it doesn't matter what anyone thinks. There is no accountability, only bank accounts, only monetary and strategic validation for unbridled, unethical deeds. There is only evil...

Here they come!

The two men tread through the forest a bit when Sophistico says, "His name is Saul...this is curious." Super Snake raises an eyebrow and says: "Now why is that?"

"Have you ever read the Holy Bible?"

"I don't trouble myself with such hindering texts."

"Well you should, regardless of your beliefs. There are things to be learned from all written and spoken word."

"Get to the point. Please."

"Well Saul, from the Bible, had an interesting end you see—shall I quote you a verse or two?"

"By all means."

> *"1 Samuel 31:4-6 Then said Saul unto his Armour bearer, Draw thy sword, and thrust me through therewith; lest these uncircumcised come and thrust me through, and abuse me. But his Armour bearer would not; for he was sore afraid. Therefore Saul took a sword, and fell upon it. And when his Armour bearer saw that Saul was dead, he fell likewise upon his sword, and died with him. So Saul died, and his three sons, and his Armour bearer, and all his men, that same day together."*

The Snake stopped in his tracks and smirked the most subtle of smirks and said: "Very curious."

To Be Continued...

Next time! On Missions!

How will Jacob respond to the decision made by Saul that led to the end of Mission two?!

Who is Luther? What is the Murrock?

Who are the assassins and what are their plans for Saul and his men?

I will tell you this!

There are some very important *players* that are entering the *game*.

Azrael, Jerusalem, Tao, Adis, Osiris, Mona, The list goes on and on!

These new players will become a big part of the even bigger picture!

This book is not what you think it is. This life is not what you think it is.

Stay faithful, and behold!...

The Truth.

THANK YOU FOR READING